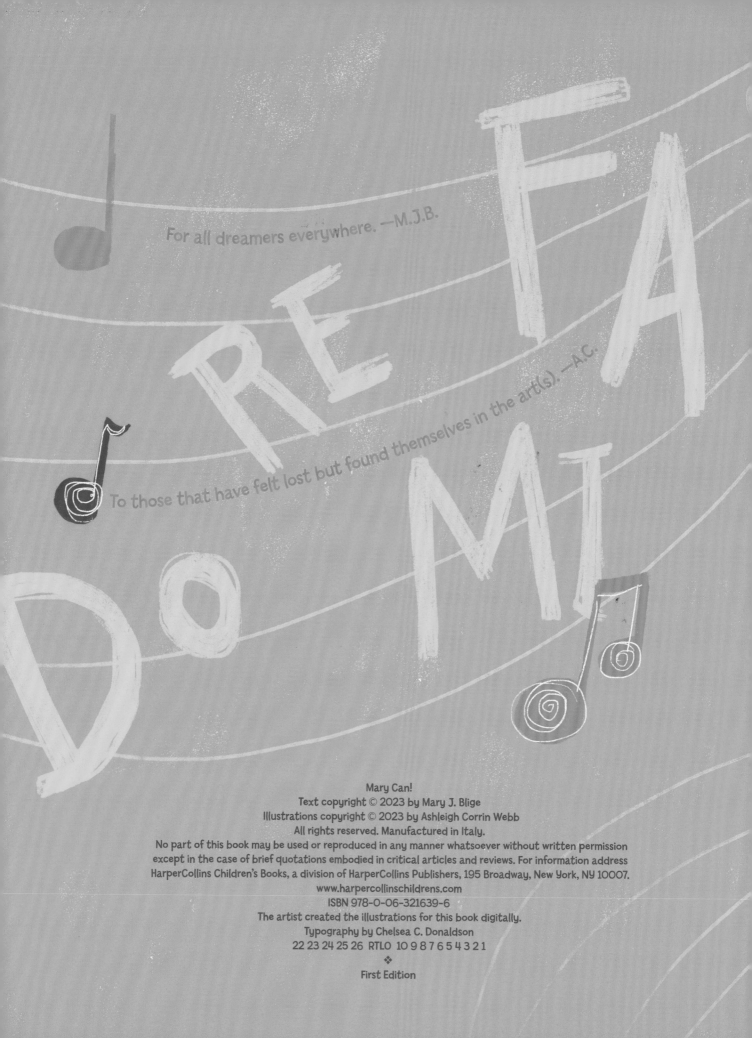

For all dreamers everywhere. —M.J.B.

To those that have felt lost but found themselves in the art(s). —A.C.

Mary Can!
Text copyright © 2023 by Mary J. Blige
Illustrations copyright © 2023 by Ashleigh Corrin Webb
All rights reserved. Manufactured in Italy.
No part of this book may be used or reproduced in any manner whatsoever without written permission
except in the case of brief quotations embodied in critical articles and reviews. For information address
HarperCollins Children's Books, a division of HarperCollins Publishers, 195 Broadway, New York, NY 10007.
www.harpercollinschildrens.com
ISBN 978-0-06-321639-6
The artist created the illustrations for this book digitally.
Typography by Chelsea C. Donaldson
22 23 24 25 26 RTLO 10 9 8 7 6 5 4 3 2 1
❖
First Edition

SO LA TI TI

Mary J. Blige

mary can!

DOOOOO

illustrated by
Ashleigh Corrin

HARPER
An Imprint of HarperCollins Publishers

I'm Mary!

I love a lot of things.

I love singing.

I love double Dutch.

And I love, love, love cooking with Grandma.

You know what I don't love, though? This one word that I happen to hear *a lot*. It starts with *n* and ends with *o*.

One more cookie?

NO!

Mismatched shoes?

NO!

Ride a two-wheeler? With my new jellies on? Please?!

You guessed it:

No. No!

And No!

But nothing beats when people find *more* words to say the *same* thing.
Like . . .

Not Yet.

Sorry, honey.

And the worst of all . . .

Yeah, I know that every day can't be a yes day.
Sometimes a no here and there is necessary.

But most of the time, people say "no" or
"you can't" because they dream too small.

I remember the first time I heard "you can't."
I was in Ms. Robinson's class. I showed up bright
and early because I was super excited.

"We're going to learn scales today," said
Ms. Robinson. "Then we will choose our lead
singer for the showcase."

I reaaally wanted to sing lead (or any part for that matter), so I made sure to practice my scales the night before. Mommy's ears were ringing, but I think I nailed it.

Singing is my absolute favorite thing! Being a singer is my dream!

I stood up tall and took a deep breath in.

And that's when I heard it.

"Mary, you CAN'T jump right into scales; you don't know them yet," Ms. Robinson said as some of the other kids giggled. "Please take your seat."

It might have been the worst CAN'T ever. I didn't even get to try. I was crushed!

After that, those two words seemed to follow me. I heard "you can't" *everywhere.*

"I want to be an astronaut!"

you can't

"I'm going to be the president!"

"I'm going to get my own star!"

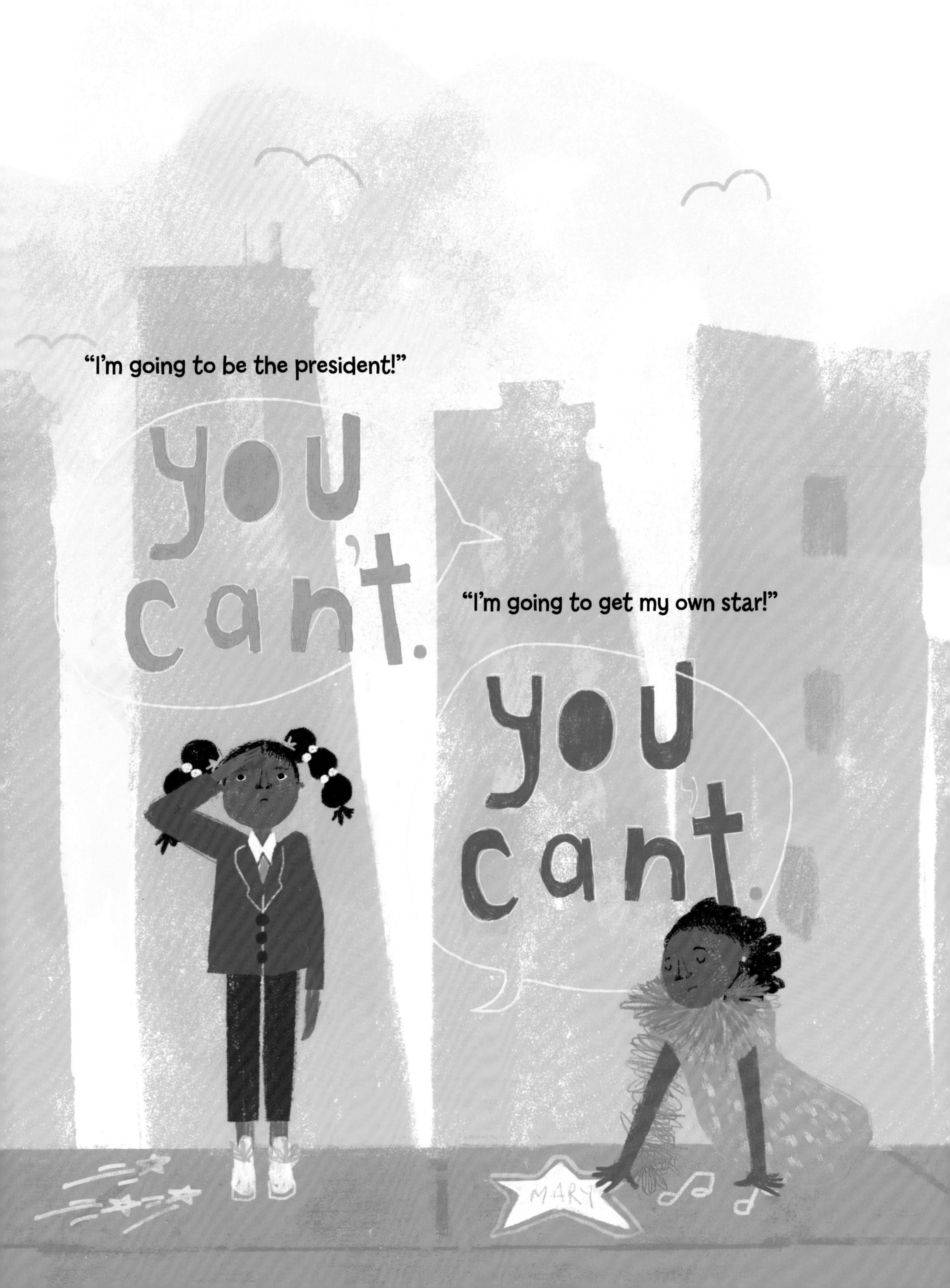

"Mommy!"

"What is it, honey? Come sit," Mommy said as she rubbed my cheek the way she always does.

"Who invented 'you can't?'" I asked. "Everyone keeps saying it to me."

"Well, I'm not sure who invented it. But when it comes to our dreams, that phrase isn't part of our family's vocabulary," Mommy said.

"It's not?" I asked.

"When have you ever seen Mommy or Grandma not do something because someone said we couldn't?" she replied.

I thought about it long and hard. Mommy and Grandma sure did a lot of things. They were unstoppable! Unflappable! Unwavering!

"Actually, never."
"Right, baby girl. Now, you take *that* to anyone who says 'you can't.'"

With Mommy's words in my heart and a new way to walk, I learned how to beat "can't" with "can."

Yes, you can.

Who can travel to space?

Who can wear mismatched
shoes to the inauguration?

mary
can!

mary
can!

Who can ride in on a two-wheeler
to pose with her shiny star?

Mary
can!

MARY

And most important, who can
work hard, follow their dreams, and
do whatever they set their mind to?

When I finally returned to Ms. Robinson's class, she said we'd be learning scales again. I pulled back and took a deeeeep breath in.

I was just about to start the warm-up, but I didn't hear the piano.

"We haven't gotten there yet, Mary; you can't learn scales overnight," Ms. Robinson said kindly.

"Would it be okay if I tried?" I asked. "Because I think I can."

tick tick tick

Ms. Robinson smiled and let
me take the floor.

DO RE
MI FA
SO LA TI

She was surprised
to say the least.

"Well, class. I think this proves that, indeed,

mary can."

Yep, I can. I sure can.

Author's Note

Mary Can! is inspired by my real life.

There was a time when I was always told that I couldn't do anything and that I was never enough.

I knew something was wrong with the words "you can't" because I knew I could! I always knew I was smart and gifted. So when I kept hearing the opposite, it was confusing.

I want you to know that if you ever hear the words "you can't," that it is not true. To all the little ones out there, I want you know that you can!

God gave us free will, the right to choose, and a multitude of gifts and talents to choose from, and sometimes people try to take that away from us because they are afraid. But that has nothing to do with you and your beliefs and dreams. You can be whatever great thing you choose!

Now, there are *some* healthy noes, so be obedient to your parents, teachers, and elders and always ask questions if you're confused or afraid about something.

But when it comes to your ambitions and goals, remove the words "can't" and "no" from your mind. Yes, you can be all you aspire to be if you believe in yourself.

Yes, mary can, and YOU can, too!

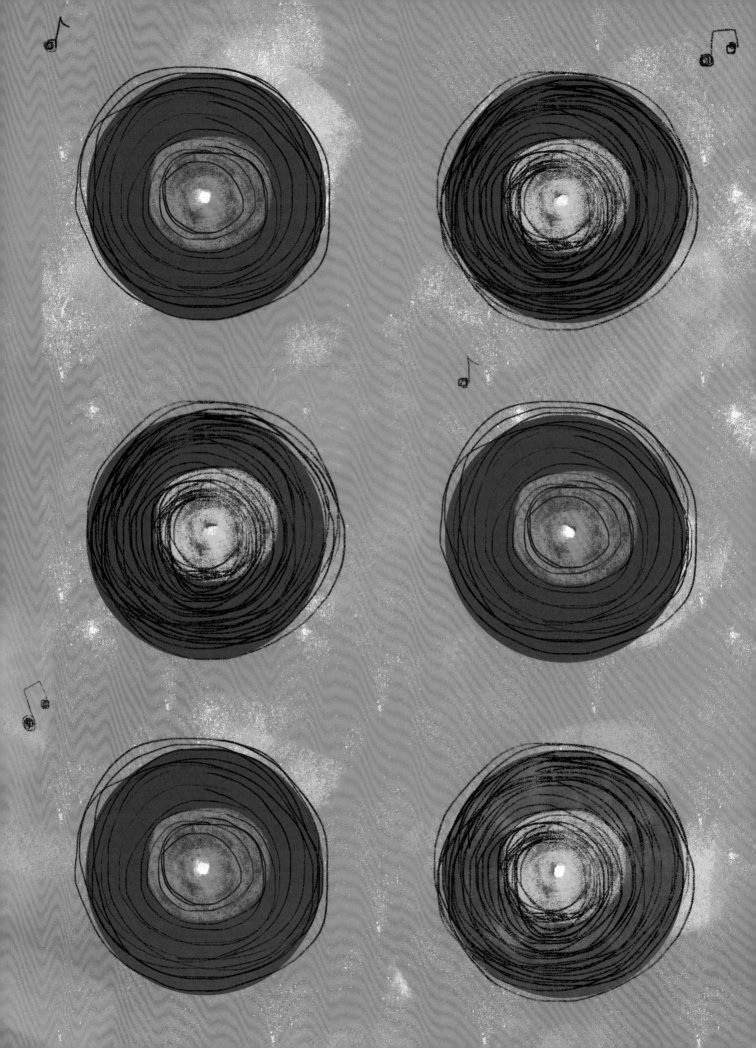